ICE AGE™
DAWN OF THE DINOSAURS

MY THREE DADS

Ice Age: Dawn of the Dinosaurs™ & © 2009 Twentieth Century Fox Film Corporation. All Rights Reserved.
First published in the UK by HarperCollins Children's Books in 2009
1 3 5 7 9 10 8 6 4 2
ISBN-13: 978-0-00-784737-2
A CIP catalogue record for this title is available from the British Library. No part of this publication may be reproduced,
stored in a retrieval system or transmitted in any form or by any means, electronic, mechanical, photocopying, recording or otherwise,
without the prior permission of HarperCollins Publishers Ltd, 77-85 Fulham Palace Road, Hammersmith, London, W6 8JB.
www.harpercollins.co.uk
Printed and bound in the UK

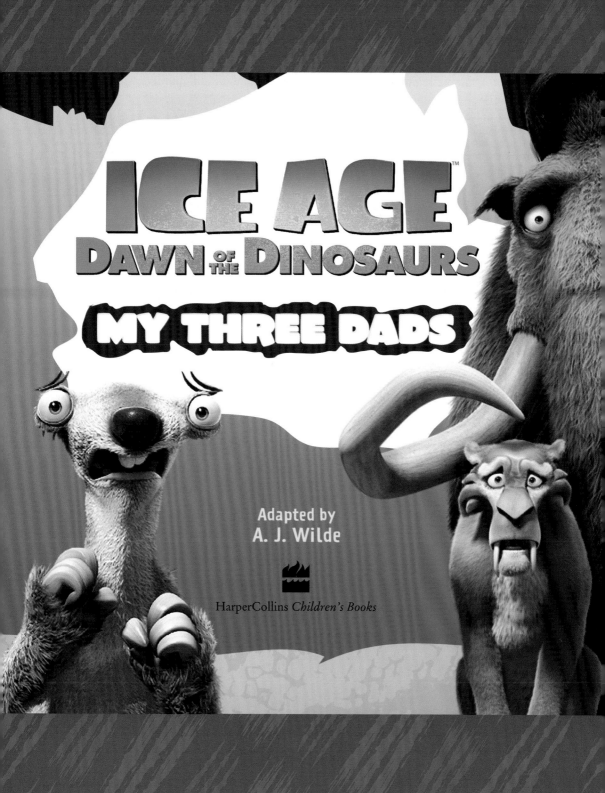

ICE AGE™
DAWN OF THE DINOSAURS
MY THREE DADS

Adapted by
A. J. Wilde

HarperCollins *Children's Books*

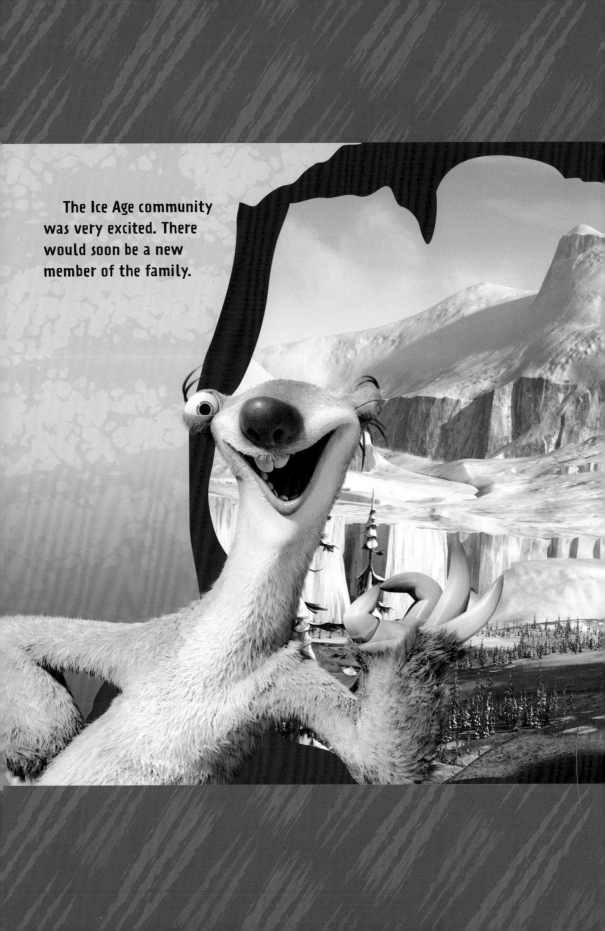

The Ice Age community was very excited. There would soon be a new member of the family.

Manny and Ellie were expecting a baby.

Sid and Diego were as excited as the mammoths about the new addition. They felt like fathers-to-be!

But, as the birth of the baby got closer, Manny started to worry. The Ice Age seemed like a very dangerous place for a little mammoth.

One day, Ellie noticed the pond near the family cave was gone. "Wasn't there a pond over here?" asked a very confused Ellie.

"I drained it," explained Manny. "A baby could drown in a pond!"

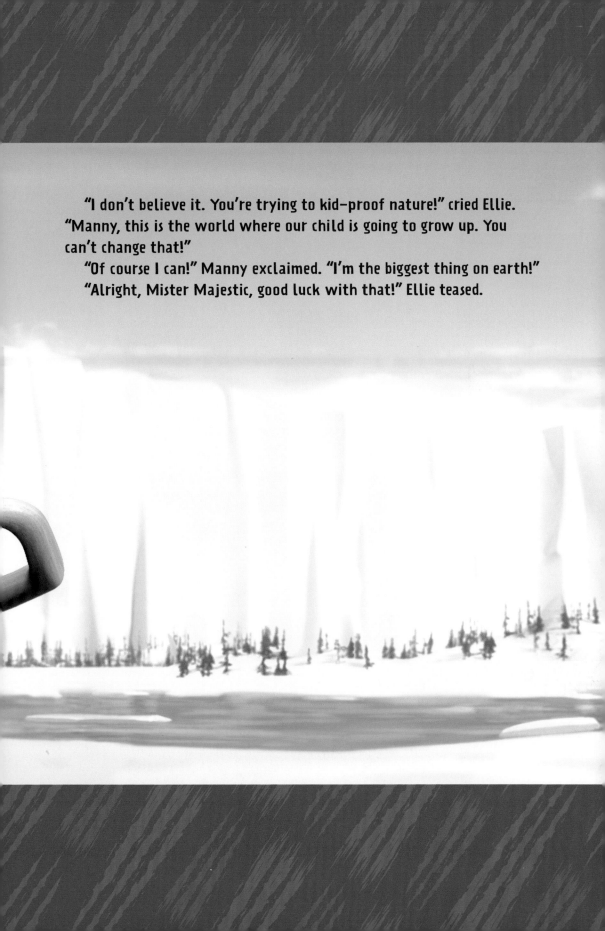

"I don't believe it. You're trying to kid-proof nature!" cried Ellie. "Manny, this is the world where our child is going to grow up. You can't change that!"

"Of course I can!" Manny exclaimed. "I'm the biggest thing on earth!"

"Alright, Mister Majestic, good luck with that!" Ellie teased.

Manny formed a plan to make their dangerous world safe for his kid — but he would need help.

As honorary dads, Sid and Diego were behind him all the way.

The three "dads" were on a mission to make the baby's world as safe and friendly as possible. They set out to change the tundra one piece of frozen danger at a time.

Sid wanted to protect his little friend from sharp branches!
He placed snowballs on their tips.

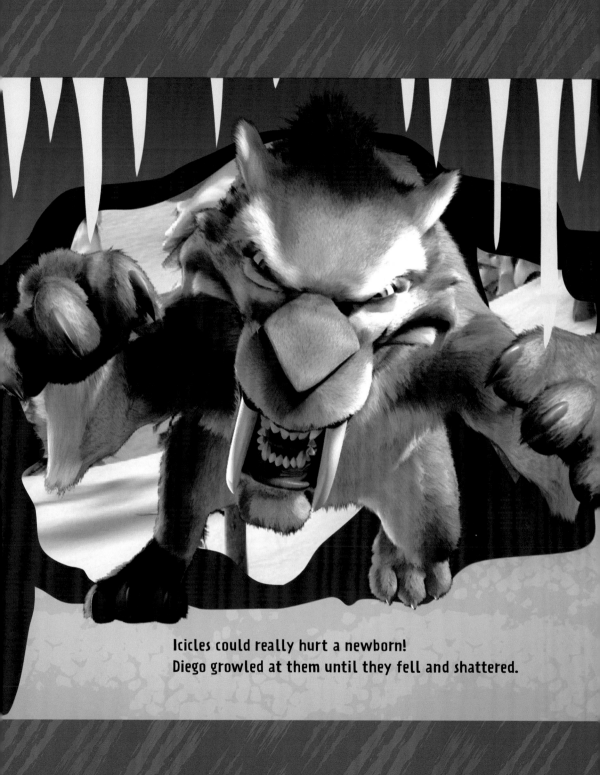

Icicles could really hurt a newborn!
Diego growled at them until they fell and shattered.

Sid wanted the baby to have somewhere comfortable to sleep. He carefully cleared away some snow to reveal soft, green grass.

When the three "dads" finished with their hard work, Manny showed Ellie what they had accomplished.

"Voila!" Manny yelled.

"Playground for Junior!" Sid declared proudly.

"Oh, Manny. It's . . . amazing! OUCH!" Ellie grabbed her belly.

"What? Is it happening?" Manny shouted.

"The baby just kicked," Ellie cried.
"The baby *kicked*!" Diego exclaimed.
"Are you okay?" Sid asked.
"Yes, and the baby is on its way!"
Ellie explained.

Manny was very excited.
He was going to be a dad at last!
"Not long to wait now," Ellie
told him.

Soon enough, baby Peaches was born, and everyone was so excited to meet her. All of a sudden, Manny worried that the ice mobile he made was dangerous. Would it fall on his baby?

"You've got to relax!" exclaimed Ellie. "The best way to protect our child is to have our friends around us."

With extra "dads" like Sid and Diego, the little mammoth would be very safe indeed.